Bones and All

BY

R.C.S

Bones and All

The floor of the restaurant was slick, poorly lit, and mostly bare except for a few elegantly made-up tables scattered like candle lit islands in the dark. The faces of the patrons remained expressionless as the three new arrivals entered. They craned their heads and arched their backs in an eerie unison that seemed to roll through the room in waves. Their clothes had suggested different times that they had come from different times and places, but their faces had begun to wear smooth to one degree or another. Some looked almost human. Others only had a sunken hole in the center of their faces and mouths filled with sucking lamprey teeth.

The grim aristocracy of their meal was contrasted by the room's other guests. Gargantuan amniotic slugs slowly slithered between each table. Their antennae twitching and scanning the air for some unseen purpose. Inside the slugs the vague outline of human bodies could be seen violently fornicating while they floated in the digestive fluids. The truth was somewhere between necrophilia and indigestion. The slugs reared up and down and occasionally seemed to writhe in ecstasy before expelling gallons of fluid onto the marble floor. Diligent busboys followed closely behind with push brooms who spread the slime evenly onto the floor.

Each of the new guests looked at the ground and stepped with careful revulsion to avoid slipping as they descended the entrance's small steps. One woman who dined alone seemed to take special note of the newcomer's arrival. You could have called her beautiful, once. She had sharp features and long legs that peeked out from the slit in her long black dress. Her hair was neatly pretzeled into a stylish updo that would be hell to wait for if you had somewhere to be. Her skin was the same color as bleached wood and had unwholesome striations that ran just under her skin like thick dark veins that stood out so starkly against her pale color. Her meal didn't stop immediately when she saw them. She only smiled with bright red lips, the only real bit of color on her and brought her fork up to her mouth as she slid the glistening piece of meat onto her tongue. She hadn't taken her eyes off them once.

The red lipped woman placed her napkin gently on the table before rising from her table to greet her guests. "Darlings, you have arrived, haven't you?" She reached out for one of her guests' hands in an almost pleasant gesture.

"Besheba" one of the three said without expression. The unwholesome Madonna contrived an expression of disappointment, but it quickly peeled back into a playful catlike malice. The three could see the energy of room rising and falling with her interest. Each strand of interconnected energy playing off one another, but all leading back to the epicenter. Their host wasn't hostile, not yet. She was bored – which could be a great deal more dangerous.

Besheba moved closer and looked with eyes that saw more than the light reflected. Eyeing each other them and plucking the fearful thoughts that lingered around the corners of their minds. Sarah. Marcus. Julia. The rest was concealed from her. There was a mist that clung around them like a halo of fog.

Sarah stepped forward and formally presented her hand "We are seekers and invoke the sacrament and protection of your master" her legs shook as she spoke the words. The room seemed to contract with pressure as the aloof staff suddenly began to rapidly set another table. Their hostess smiled with gleeful malice as she placed a fingertip on Sarah's arm "You're so formal. We could just call this a favor between friends"

"We don't know what a favor costs in the end" Marcus said bluntly. Besheba only smiled with her mouth as she almost hissed "You'd have to ask the empty seats darling." It pulled a seat from the perfectly groomed table and gestured with he other hand "But please, be my guests"

"I'm really not very hungr-" The words had barely come out of Marcus' mouth when Besheba spun around. Her dress writhed as if there were unseen appendages that flailed in anger beneath the silk fabric "YOU WILL EAT!!!" their host screamed while the patrons at the table grabbed the sides of their heads and howled in agony and rage.

Sarah's mask of emotionlessness cracked as she turned and looked at Marcus in disbelief. Their hosts composed herself instantly and held out her slender arm towards a table and beamed "Welcome to the Farthest Shore"

The hall swooned with attention as the table settings were laid out. The massive slugs seemed to drift closer to the epicenter of the new stimulus and even the aloof diners who still had eyes let them wander sideways. Sarah waited until Besheba walked away for a moment to supervise the meals preparation and she quickly rattled off a warning to Marcus and Julia "Keep something repulsive in mind, no matter what you can't enjoy this meal. Focus on something nauseating."

A massive fuck slug shivered behind Sarah and violently expelled another pressurized blast of fluids onto the floor behind it. Marcus winced reflexively and said "Yes. I think I can do that" with mournful confidence.

"And what the fuck happens if we can't?!" Julia barked a loud whisper at Sarah. The three of them turned as the sound of squelching moans escaped one of the slug's sphincter orifices with slow unspeakable understanding.

"Darlings! Dinner is served" Besheba almost sang the words.

The three sat tensely as their hostess orchestrated the movement around them as glasses of wine were poured and utensils were perfectly arranged around their plates. Julia could smell the semi-sweet odor that drifted out of the wine glass in front of her. "Don't like wine?" Besheba asked genuinely curious. "No, not really but it smells delicious" Julia answered honestly.

"It does, doesn't it?" Besheba smiled as if she had been complimented, and joked as she passed Sarah a glass "She's already more popular than you here Sarah"

"It's your feast isn't it deep-spawn" Sarah's voice was even and without emotion as she said the words. Besheba's lips tightened for a moment but then softened back into an easy smile as she said, "You're so right about that."

Besheba started to walk away but stopped and put her hand on Sarah's shoulder and said with at least some sincerity "I love that we haven't dropped the dinner metaphors" Besheba's whispered the next part politely like gossip at a wedding, but her eyes were murderous and without human feeling as she looked back at them "Bon Appetit"

 The charcuterie board was placed at the center of the table. The arrangements were carefully laid out rows of rich looking cured meats, odd colored cheeses, and dried fruits. The waiters were dressed in traditional white tail suits and moved with such a practiced familiarity that it almost looked choreographed. A spectacle only further magnified by the server's complete lack of facial features, each one provided service without the benefits of eyes, mouths, or ears. Like a horror show Fregoli Delusion come to life.

 Julia looked across the table at Sarah as she cautiously placed her napkin in her lap and frantically tried to recall any niceties that were appropriate in an upscale restaurant. Marcus began to pick small pieces of fruit off the tray even before the staff had finished setting it down on the table. Sarah nodded her head at the tray and Julia understood that their participation was not voluntary.

 They each picked up a few different kinds of meats and cheeses. Marcus put a piece of what looked like cured beef in his mouth, but the taste was much sweeter and gamy - crusted with herbs that lingered around and augmented the natural flavors and salts that ran through the meat. He closed his eyes and immediately received a kick in the shin as Sarah immediately growled quietly "Stop enjoying the food Marcus!" He rubbed his leg and began to chew again slowly while he cast sour looks at Sarah, who in return looked at Marcus like he'd perpetually shit in her bed.

Marcus looked contrite he stopped before he took another bite and asked, "Sorry it's just good - is it venison?" Sarah looked at him gravely and visibly forced herself to take another bite "It's closet to pig."

There was the sound of teeth as they drug down the tines of forks. The noise was amplified in those quiet lulls between the horrid sucking noises made by the fuck slugs as the inched across the floor. Lipstick on wine glasses and exposed shoulders. Multiple points of penetration multiplied by dozens of participants on polished marble floors. The reflection of everything was distorted and unfocused in the imperfect mirror under them - the only thing worse than the reality.

Sarah took a moment between bites and focused her mind on the truth behind the meal. Passed the refined menu and the discordant moans of the slugs. Down the hall with Della Francesca paintings, carefully curated and lit so each crack and brushstroke served in perfect harmony to the restaurant's diabolical good taste. Behind the white doors and through the kitchens, immaculate and organized. A collection of pristine sharp edges on display in the freezers. Though the door isn't hidden, no one dares go through it. Down the stone steps, blackened by the great fire. The stone rooms in the dark and splattered depths, hung from hooks to plead, still alive, left to die in a place with no light.

They were led to the freight elevators, but their host didn't try and hide her disappointment. "Sarah, I think you'll find our side of the agreement here more than adequate, wouldn't you agree?"

Sarah didn't bother to respond as she got onto the lift. Besheba rolled her eyes and turned as she closed the steel grate door. She held fixed her eyes on Sarah before she asked, "A piece of advice if I could?"

"If you must" Sarah said full of food and contempt.

"You should stay up here - you and your friends should stay and have a drink." Besheba leaned forward on the elevator gate pressed herself up against it like they'd danced all night "Up here it's only unpleasant if you fight it." She waited a few moments for a response before she shrugged her shoulders and sent the elevator down. She looked at them all as they descended below "Down there it's always unpleasant." Besheba sighed as the elevator began to descend and pressed her red lips against the grates as they descended into the dark.

Scrubland

All magic comes from fear. You're at the edge of something - it might be a pit or a mountain. Impossible to cross blind, so you light the first candles to see it better. To witness the stalking revelation in the flesh. But the candles aren't enough. They can only illuminate the edges of that terrible implication. Those little lights of yours are not nearly bright enough to cross the face of the deep. The words come next. Self- assuring and filled with the confidence of inexperience. They echo into the dark and anchor, like hooks, a sense of distance. They're temporary or maybe just meaningless. Like the last particles of starlight at the end of the universe. The billions of lonely motes fleeing the inevitable.

You can hear the dark cooing now, as the first drops are spilled. The first cuts are reluctant, gentle. You've teased it from the farthest places imaginable and dim ruddy illumination begins to brew in the dark. The pit begins to speak and like the first time you hear the words 'I love you' you want more. Those drops have become a gush now. The meaning has anchored but there is an uncertainty. A question of who's being pulled. All hesitation is gone. A path has begun to form - how could you have missed it? Your hands are wet now, clothes stuck to the front of your chest like a night after a near fatal fever. You're ankle deep in the truth. You began down the path without the realization that you'd even begun, and every moment that passes greater torrents are needed.

There are others, stranded along the side of the labyrinth walls. From other times and places. Those who have come before and some that are yet to be born. All share the shade of a place that cannot be. Their faces are frozen with the terror of the answer to their questions, skin calcified like the grey ashen walls that surround you. The light from their hearts the only tell that the state of their existence is one of conscious living torture. They glow inside their rent chests, rib cages held open by their rictus hands.

Did you begin this with someone? They're gone now. Swept away in the flood of knowledge. Lost in it, or to it. It's just you, a flickering thing. The path seems to go on forever, and every turn reveals the greater danger ahead. Sit now. Sit now and rest against the cool stones. Let your fingers slip beneath the facade of your skin. Pull apart the troublesome sinew and bone. Someone will be along soon. Let the light of your heart guide them to you - wait just a little while in the dark.

Dangerous Habits

"We can do this." The words came out thick with anxiety. She held the leather-bound book close to her chest like it was a found child. Her friend Annie walked a few steps behind her as they came down the old stone steps of the school's chapel. They crossed the courtyard and Sarah felt the dour eyes of the Virgin Mary watch them as they snuck across the rough flagstone walkway, barefoot. She clutched the book tighter and peeked around the corner of the library building to see if anyone was awake to catch them out of bed.

They scurried past the pastor's apartments and could see a single light burning on the second floor. It was sickly and yellow - bleeding through the white curtains with a jaundiced aura of infection. Annie nudged her in the back, and they continued to the old, perforated metal steps behind the cafeteria - the way that led down to the school's fallout shelter. It was part of the original building, from that time before it was a school - when no one came there to learn anything but to keep quiet reverently. Like everything else there, it had been repurposed.

The steel door at the bottom of the steps was heavy and old, almost completely rusted out. Its color was the same as a scab on a dry day. Sarah bit the tip of her thumb and felt her incisor break through the skin with a sharp rush of pain. She smeared the blood on the door in an intricate pattern that formed as much in her mind as on the pitted iron. It dried in the hot summer air and the metal almost looked thirsty as the blood faded into the color of the ruddy, uneven surface. She imagined how old the locks were, and every crack that could've formed in their fragile tumblers from decades of neglect. She saw the bolts that held up the door that could've loosened from a maintenance man's rough shoulder check months before. The pry bar he might've used when it failed to budge. How he might've even forgotten to lock it behind him when he'd finished his work that day. Sarah took a single finger and imagined all the ways that the door could've failed to keep them out. It seemed only natural when the rusted lock cracked and fell to the floor, completely shattered.

"Annie, you have to remember what I said, yeah?" The younger girl nodded her head, but the doubt was palpable. They had found the book down in the basement library with all of the outdated liturgical texts, still lost in superstitions about history, race, and science. Anne started to say something, but the dingy basement floor was so cold compared to the courtyard that it stole the words from her and escaped only as a shallow gasp.

Sarah had begun her preparations a week earlier. Abstinence from different foods and drinks were necessary parts of the book's instructions. It all made her feel queasy - the grit on the floor and being entombed by iron and concrete on all sides. They had drifted underneath the school - below the surface of the world. She had read the words without much difficulty. They spoke as much as they were seen - they hissed softly when observed carefully. A halting, sharp font like daggers pointed at the reader.

Annie was a few years younger than Sarah - just at the edge of the larger part of her life. Her hair was sandy blonde, with thin wisps of sun-bleached platinum. Sarah watched her friend's bare feet move across the floor. She thought they still moved like little girls, without the careful fear that would come later. They had to duck down to reach the storage room, through the narrow concrete steps beneath the stairs leading up. The old wooden access door was squat and gray from a century of cold condensation and apathy.

Beyond was the hallway that led to the fallout shelter. Pipes lined both sides of the passage and left everything wet with a slick and oily moisture. It felt like the entrails of the school. It was necessary. The appointed place needed to be secluded - their worship had to be hidden from the eyes of everyone. Everything had to be just so.

Their path dead ended in the decayed remnants of the school's shelter. An old wood burning boiler sat prominently in the center of the room. Old black iron pipes led up and out of the room through the ceiling, to carry away the choking smoke. Some of the older students had heard about this place. It was the ghost story that every old place had - they called it the black room there. Students were taken down into the dark to have their hands branded on the red-hot furnace. A place of punishment seemed appropriate. Sarah imagined that it was but shuddered to think of what else might have happened in that room. The place where god couldn't see.

Sarah fumbled nervously in her bag for the components that she'd manage to scrounge together over the last month. She could feel every nervous tremble in her fingers as she laid out each carefully prepared element onto the concrete floor. She paused to take a breath after a near false start had shaken her confidence even further. She didn't exhale for two heartbeats, not until she had placed the photo of Father McKenna at the center of her rite. There was a moment of guilt that came when she looked at his photo one last time, a sense that she held some responsibility for everything that had happened. She let it slip past and replaced it with her anger at not having acted sooner. She set aside her motives and produced a stained piece of chalk from a small wooden jewelry box. The chalk had been sealed in oak and drowned in a virgin's blood on the night of a new moon. They didn't have much of what they needed, and she knew it would be another month before they could try it again if she screwed up. Her skin crawled at the thought. Another month and it might be impossible altogether - there might not be a virgin left at the school.

She chased the distraction from her mind and felt the chalk's edge bite down on the rough texture of the dirty floor. A complex pattern began to form on the stone around the spell's components. Her hand moved with a certainty that she hadn't expected. Each curve and line formed fully in her mind before it ever found its way onto the ground. The symbols were static, but they had their mirror image behind her closed eyelids. They broke apart in her imagination - reformed into sharp wire and rigid bars around the father's face. A cage of rusty metal and malice. She watched the vision of his features become marred as the grid that surrounded him pressed tightly against his skin. The cage grew smaller and drew trickles of blood from his face in small square patterns. It pushed the compressed flesh out from each box in small pseudopods of rupturing skin and burst blood vessels. The intent of her working was a screaming box of hair and flesh in her mind. The photo in the circle had become his holy card - it bled and cracked sharply in a pattern that mimicked her desire.

"Sarah…" Annie had let her voice float meekly into the carnage of the moment. She said something, but it was far away. Some part of Sarah had understood the words. A warning or a plea to stop maybe. Sarah responded absently, but her voice had become two - and in a diabolical harmony they both said flatly "**No**". Sarah could hear something. It sounded like a terrible groan that made the room shiver. Close to the feeling of a finger that unexpectedly runs along the surface of your skin. Annie's hands covered her ears - she backed against the wall. Sarah couldn't be bothered. The room had sunk back into that crypt like the silence they'd found it in. She could only hear her two voices.

The altar candles had melted completely, but the wicks remained suspended upright. They burned with surprising intensity - but they didn't seem to give off much illumination. Sarah could see Annie's face, but indistinctly. Her friend's eyes were wide, and her cheeks flushed. Like she was holding her breath. Sarah kept the ritual going, the book had explained very clearly that it would be far worse for them if she stopped after she started. The magic would demand its victim, and it didn't matter who.

Sarah couldn't hear anything except the sounds of the words as she spoke them. The will and the intent formed in her mind as one entity. Annie was up against the wall, almost on her toes, head arched back in some silent spasming seizure. She tried to say something. She looked at Sarah and her eyes pleaded. The candles couldn't light the room anymore. Everything hovered at the edge of nonexistence.

The words were everything. Pipes around them had begun to shake and fall from their moorings in the walls. The shadows on the floor from the candles deepened and elongated up and around them - even as the light that was cast from them pulsed and fluttered as though struggling to breathe. Sarah could only hear the words. Each sound and syllable mimed in perfect time by another deeper, and more hateful speaker. She turned to look at Annie. The darkness felt like the haze of a blinding heat. It twisted what she could make out at the edge of their light. Another person was in the room with them, but she couldn't make out their features. Only the rough silhouette of another small form with long dark hair. They stood close to Annie. Close enough to hear a secret. Sarah tried to stop - she clenched her fists and took one feeble step before the words asserted themselves again. She could feel the tension of her muscles as they began to cramp from the force of her effort to move. Her face was hot and every tear that streamed down her cheeks felt like an icy razor.

The other voice was louder now. It had crawled from her throat and hung in the air like a pestilence. It drifted up and down the walls and coated every surface with the profane. It tongued everything until it finally settled above the other in the room. It didn't come from them exactly, but it drifted above their head and swirled like an echoed nightmare. A crown of hate. She didn't have to see it now to know who it was supposed to look like. Whose hair and skin it wore while it strangled her friend. She was glad that the light was almost gone now. She didn't want to see its face. She didn't want to see how much it enjoyed itself as it choked the life from someone she loved.

The words continued as two but formed as one terrible utterance. The space between the words Sarah spoken and the words unspoken by the other. The candles fluttered one last time as the spell finished. She didn't have to see its face to feel its smile. Sarah's voice broke free first as the room sank into nothingness. It was a ragged scream of animal terror and the herald of a shattered heart.

WHERE THE WOODS END

With this excellent resolve for the future, Goodman Brown felt himself justified in making more haste on his present evil purpose. He had taken a dreary road, darkened by all the gloomiest trees of the forest, which barely stood aside to let the narrow path creep through, and closed immediately behind. It was all as lonely as could be; and there is this peculiarity in such a solitude, that the traveler knows not who may be concealed by the innumerable trunks and the thick boughs overhead; so that with lonely footsteps he may yet be passing through an unseen multitude. "There may be a devilish Indian behind every tree," said Goodman Brown to himself; and he glanced fearfully behind him as he added:

What if the devil himself should be at my very elbow?

She hadn't gotten used to the room yet. They had let her sleep in their room for too long and now to get her to sleep in her own bed was going to be a hard transition. It was the third time he'd come to check on her, each time her little saccharine pout waited expectantly for reassurance and comfort. He'd start the investigation with the closet-slowly opened the door in mock sus pense and conducted a careful search of the toy chests and the neatly folded clothes.

"No monsters here sweetie" trying his best serious detective face before he closed the doors and continued the search in other suspicious locales around the room. He looked behind the heavy blue and white curtains, and inside the footlocker at the edge of her bed. Each time he would turn back to smile and watch her little eyelids struggle against inevitable. Finally, he'd climb down on all fours and lift the duvet covers that hung over the edge of the bed and stare into the clandestine dark underneath-his smart phone flashlight used industriously to chase the shadows back revealed nothing but the bare wooden floors. Before he was on his feet again she was fast asleep, the little cadence of her breath rose and fell with deep slumber. He stood for a few minutes and watched her sleep- made sure that a spasm of fitful ness wouldn't jar her awake again and begin the nightly ritual anew.

There was something about the room though-he could see it from her perspective. It was almost as large as the master bedroom, but more sparsely furnished to accommodate whatever play she might get up to. It made the whole thing seem a bit lonely at night, and he thought maybe it might do to buy her a dog or a cat to keep her company. He picked up a little as he backed out quietly and took a small pile of books from the floor and returned them to their proper place on the bookshelf next to the window. He stared for a moment at his backyard and let his eyes wander back and forth and looked for nothing. His home sat on the edge of a ticky-tacky subdivision that was never truly completed. Never lived in homes sat unused kept only by the cleaners and landscapers, employed by the bank who owned the properties, trawled the neighborhood bi-monthly.

The east side of the house overlooked a half-formed ghost town and the west, where his little girl's room sat, faced the overgrown woods that crept up to the edge of their property. He never liked wilderness, not that the bare woods that grew around them could be called wilderness, walk an hour in those woods and you'd hit a major road, but still he couldn't help hate the idea of her getting lost even for a little while out there. There was a slight breeze that blew in and rustled the curtains, and though he knew it was nothing he still closed the window. He closed the window and stared at the skeletal trees as they twitched and swayed slightly in the wind.

He didn't shut the door behind him as he walked slowly into the well-lit hallway. It was close to 3:15 in the morning but he didn't feel tired. He headed down the stairs and into the living room and took a seat in the center of the couch. He let the television chatter idly in the background while he waited for his body to want rest again and wished that his mind could slow down enough to let him relax. But his thoughts again drifted out in into the wilderness. He had always hated the woods he admitted, even when he was a kid, camping had always filled him with a sense of vague anxiety. He supposed there isn't really any other kind but vague. He knew that the edges of the map had been filled in, but you couldn't look out over the trees and not suspend your disbelief for a second-there was al ways something invasive about nature. The woods always seemed to be lurking on the just on the outskirts of everything known-it lived on the very edge of small towns and rural roads and didn't just wait, but with a long silent vigil… seemed to wait with purpose.

He could hear her tossing and turning in bed again, he sighed and smiled as he got up. He'd only gotten about three hours of sleep and he'd need to be up for work again in a few more. He turned the dial on the stove and watched the pure blue flames click in a small burst. He filled his wife's teapot, placed it on the burner, and produced from the pantry sugar and teabags. Years earlier he'd been introduced to the English style of milk in tea, but as he opened the carton the sickly smell of spoiled dairy smashed into his nose like a clenched fist.

A loud thud came from upstairs, and he was immediately sure that she'd fallen from her bed again. He turned off the stove and ascended the stairs a slow exhausted trudge. A peek into the room revealed nothing out of the ordinary; she still slept soundly cocooned in her blankets and cartoonishly snored. He walked around the upstairs and checked the other rooms. The house was so asleep-even the groans of protest from the wooden floor under his bare feet seemed groggy. He satisfied himself that everything was in order before he headed downstairs again, and again carefully began to make complete his pot of tea and attempt to start his Saturday hideously early. He dropped the carton of spoiled milk into the garbage and imagined the satisfaction he'd feel while his son took out the trash later while the tendrils of that smell wafted up at him: take that sleeping family.

Again, a thud from upstairs, he switched off the burner again, but with less amusement than the last time. He opened the door to her room again to find her sitting up in bed smiling sweetly at him. "What are you doing up pretty girl?" he couldn't help but ask with faux irritation. She shook her head and laughed quietly but didn't try and answer his rhetorical question. She pointed to the closet with the bemused gesture of a game that

had no winners but insomnia. He laughed and checked the closet again but did so with a cavalier melodrama. He flung the curtains aside in assumed a 1920's pugilist stance to battle whatever monster might spring forth. She began to restrain her mirth putting her hands over her mouth as she shook with amusement. She smiled wide and pointed with concern under the bed. He produced his smart phone again and, on all fours, lifted the duvet covers and used it as a flashlight again to chase away the familiar obscurity.

His daughter's face was wet with tears as her eyes implored with an almost hysterical fear as she lay curled up on the floor. His blood froze and after what seemed like an eternity as she whispered:

"Daddy…help…there's someone on my bed."

A Mouse's Repetition

A few years ago, we caught a mouse in a trap in a cabinet underneath the counter. It was on the shelf just above the translucent plastic breadbox. The metal spring trap had snapped down unevenly on the mouse's head and pushed one of its eyes out of its head, not completely, but enough to make the whole of the thing grotesque and pitiful looking. It's back legs scrambled with the arrival of fresh panic - the giants had come.

There was a short and sad discussion about how best to deal with the tiny living thing caught in a human's average everyday death trap. The injuries were obviously enough to end its life, if not soon at least soon after. Proximity and timing make most guilty choices inevitable.

The yellow rubber gloves slipped over my hands with some difficultly. A little sweat had begun to run on my hands and the friction it created was a merciful delay of the end of the road for all involved. I did my best to support its back as I lifted it off the pressboard shelf. It was so alive while calculating mousely methods of escape with the all the determination instinct provided it.

It was small and terrified - powerless to change its world. The late November snow clung to the ground in sparse dispersals and small pockets of green were preserved underneath. The winter had come quickly and frozen life still in that moment of sunlight of before.

I placed the trap and my new acquaintance on the ground as gently as I could. We'd only just met but sometimes you just understand someone right from the start. His eye seemed to leap out as the instrument of his heart. There was some rough thing in my hand. It had been nearby and seemed to fit too well into the casual machinery of the end of a life. I'd been outside long enough to feel the chill begin to settle and linger on my skin. Numb pins and needle pricks danced on my forearms. His eye was a straight line through me. Constant, but without accusation. He didn't have an axe to grind but every piece of him wanted the waters to turn back. Everything was too cold. The ground and the rock in my hand were cold and empty things these awful sinkholes of warmth.

My hand carefully lifted the wire from his head without my permission. The compression rose off him and the blood clearly rushed back to all his extremities in a disorientating wave. He struggled to roll off his side and took a few blackout drunk steps away, just away.

If there's a universal spirit, I hope it was watching and the memory of the moment comes back to it the next time it clenches a rock in its fist. If not, then I hope the mice stay with that mothefucker forever.

June 2012, Poi Phet Cambodia

No one told me that visas expire. It was my first time in Asia and no one told me. I was living in Bangkok for the summer sticking to the furniture of an un-air conditioned three flat apartment converted into one of the worst hostels on the face of the earth. My roommates and coworkers were fringe criminals hiding out from the authorities living for free in exchange for room and board. L was a trans woman who had escaped Myanmar on foot at the age of 8 to avoid being sold into slavery by the border military units. She wore pink wigs and oversized sunglasses but had crossed that jungle on foot alone as a child - and there was a violence and survivalism underneath the glam rock aesthetic. You could feel it moving beneath the surface.

B was a Georgian war vet who had ended up in Bangkok after a Russian soldier had stabbed him in the heart during the invasion of 2008. The details of his military service were murky all I knew was that he was on leave for an extended period going somewhere on 4 years at that point. He didn't speak much but would smoke endlessly and always wanted bread with every meal no matter how inappropriate. On the nights where he wasn't having loud sex in the bunk above me he would lock himself in the communal showers and scream until he'd had enough alcohol to pass out.

They were not ideal roommates on paper, but you make friends on the edge and do the best you can with what you have.

We'd gotten on a bus at 5 in the morning to take a visa run for me into Cambodia to reset my time in Thailand and avoid paying any exit fines at the end of my trip. My university hadn't paid me a dime yet of my monthly stipend, so we pooled some cash we already had and skimmed the rest from the till for a few days beforehand until we had enough to make the trip comfortably.

The bus was filthy, and we ended up sitting on the floor because of the fleas infesting the cushions of the seats. We played cards and chatted while driving through what might have been countryside. If it wasn't for the soul desiccating heat and the constant threat of parasitic infestation it might've been peaceful.

We had no difficulty crossing the border despite looking the part of three remorseless fugitives. I was questioned briefly by a soldier after taking a photo of one of the large intricate wooden carvings of a lion hanging on one on the wall as we entered. Our language barrier was so severe that a minute or two into the attempted interrogation he slumped his shoulders and simply trailed off mid-sentence. It was already a country on the same page as me. Exhausted from the effort and willing to let bygones be bygones if someone would volunteer a little god damn peace and quiet in its day.

We found a liquor store a few minutes after crossing the border and a dry curb to sit on in front of it. We spent the remainder of the morning drinking inexpensive beer and people watching in the hot sun. People watching is the answer we give when we're too ashamed to admit we weren't doing anything out of sheer apathetic laziness.

There was a red dust everywhere and on everything that day (possibly for all time) and it made the whole experience feel like a western. We made our way to the north of the city on foot looking for something interesting or at least predictable to eat. Collectively we decided that we'd had enough city living by midafternoon and decided to explore the green areas just outside the city. We crossed a large, tilled field and start making our way down to the nearest shady tree line.

It wasn't all at once that I even noticed that there was a man screaming at us. I'd been in Asia long enough to know that sometimes people were just screaming. But the persistence of his waiving had an unwholesome urgency to it. The other two had been drifting in an out of the moment but I was suddenly aware of everything around us. A large sign to my left about 25 yards away prominently featured a leering jawless skull. Below in several different languages, the largest being English, were the words "DANGER MINES"

We froze in absolute surreal concern. I won't say terror, but we we certainly giving the mines a long hard think. It was too surreal to be scary at first - the man had left in a hurry, and we all agreed that it would be a great favor to us if he alerted whatever authorities handled that sort of thing. But we didn't know - we kept looking at each other hoping that somewhere in the tangle of dead ends was a way out.

If you've never stood in an open field fearing for your life, there isn't an accurate way to describe how much is going on if you're forced to stand still in one spot. In a state near a total panic everything registers. You can hear and see the movement of every tiny thing in the air and on the ground and they all sound like their talking shit to you. We waited almost an hour before the Cambodian regulars made their way onto the scene. Police and a very friendly Australian minesweeper named Blake arrived a few hours later.

The police immediately shook us down for all the money we had on us. We didn't speak Cambodian, but the tone and volume of our hosts indicated that we were a costly disruption to their day. They arrested us and placed us in the back of a tiny compact police car with chicken wire separating us from the officers. I remember thinking that it was pretty good-sized town, and a proper police car didn't seem like an expense I would've tried to be thrifty about.

They drove us to the border and escorted us through the check point and back into Thailand without so much as a word. We felt lucky that they hadn't tried to keep our passports. Even with the bribe and our cheerful relief at not staining the trees with gore, their disposition never softened.

Unceremoniously dumped on the Thai border, we hitchhiked to a hospital down the road to call our employer to let him know that we were going to be late for work and explained that we needed to borrow 100 dollars US if he expected any of us to be on time the next day.

July 4th 2020, Indiana, precise location unknowable

Taking drugs in a public space is challenging on a good day. You have to filter everything you do through a scaffolded system of normalcy erected in a state of absolute insanity. I had chosen Indiana on the 4th of July to take three times the recommended dose of a psychoactive substance. More than 100 miles from home and surrounded by intolerable Hoosiers on a baking July afternoon, I ignored the angels of my better nature and let Satan take the wheel.

I'd built my tolerance up over the pandemic. So I felt confident in my ability to manage what I knew was going to be a cycle of fucked up mutating rednecks and stigmata blood pouring from every wall. I waded into the water as the foreign objects in my bloodstream started to interfere with my perceptions. Slow but significant hue changes made the lake look impossibly green and blue. Metallic and roiling with every conceivable mystery underneath. I walked slowly until submerged completely. My friends shouted from the beach, worried that in my altered state of consciousness I might do something stupid and end up another bloated corpse on the banks of Lake Michigan.

But there wasn't really any danger of that. The cold water had a pacifying effect on the trip and for a little while on the climb up there was real quiet as I surfaced and dived slowly beneath the calm dark waves.

I emerged from the water already sitting in the backseat of the car with no recollection of leaving the beach. I'm sure it was average. It was night and the fireworks had started. The explosions weren't as graceful as I would've hoped - the concussive force I felt in my chest from each burst was enough to make my heart race. My hands had begun to tremble - we were over the giddy upward ascent The light from each volley lingered too long after it'd finished and the sky was starting to become a nauseous iridescent whirlpool of color.

I struggled for a solution to the way I was feeling and decided that if I had some control over the when the explosives went off I might feel less anxious. I convinced my friends to stop at a fireworks stand - there was some bargaining and it was agreed on that we would stop but I would not be allowed to light anything purchased.

The first fireworks depot we hit was so crowded that I couldn't even see the register, much less get in line. I asked a clerk if the motors Id selected were loud and he responded

"Real talk, those are ignorantly loud" one for the record books.

Their entire set up was an open-faced sandwich of pyromaniacs, holiday drunks and exhausted parents. They were all crowded together without masks and shouting inches from each other's faces. I could hear their perspiration and greasy hair follicles rubbing together. It was in my nose and crawling down my throat like a tarantula. A nameless Hell themed like a store. No registers and no escape. I put the mortars down and tried to look calm as I walked out.

The second fireworks store went much worse.

Krazy Kaplans combines the worst elements of a 2nd amendment gun club, middle eastern bazaar and police officer meet and greet. There were logos for the store on every wall and for those of you lucky enough not to know it features a man deep into a serious meth addiction holding a lit stick of dynamite in his hand while cosplaying as Uncle Sam. His bloodshot bug eyes were on every inch of unused space and whenever I lingered to long when I looked at one, I could hear the wet sound of his protruding tongue moving.

There were hundreds of mosquitoes inside the building. Any time you stopped for too long in any one spot you could expect a swarm of them to descend on any area of exposed flesh. It felt like a sales strategy because I hadn't really bothered to check the price for a single item I'd grabbed.

There was a cop in every aisle as I randomly selected fireworks. I hadn't bothered to grab a cart or a basket but instead struggled to hold everything in my arms while I tried to avoid the Krazy Kaplan's logo from putting the evil eye on me. When I got to register the clerk asked for an id. A police officer in military style boots and riot control gear stood behind him with his hands inside the vest pockets like some dipshit napoleon.

My suspicion of self-identification became a deal breaker, and I dropped all the fireworks on the floor and left without so much as a word. Somehow, I walked past my friends who were guarding the door.

We were almost denied entry in the gentleman's club because of my sleeveless shirt. Even losing grip on what was real and what wasn't I had the presence of mind to be offended that somehow my clothes didn't measure up to that armpit fart factory of broken dreams and sweat. I had to borrow the 35 dollars necessary to purchase some of the clubs branded merchandise. I was a lean 159lb at the time and all they had were 5XL t-shirts that wore like my father's t-shirt when I was 5.

I sat in front of the stage watching purple and red-light machines bend and warble reality around them. Birthday cake of death. Someone had given me a lukewarm Miller Lite and it felt a little like bottom. The dancer on stage moved too quickly and her limbs bent in impossible demonic ways. She turned and looked at us after a pole spin and her face recessed into her skull like her face was caving in on itself. All around me all I could see was meat. There was never a moment in my life that I wished more that I had gone to school for accounting. Been the kind of man who could account. Be counted on. The world was a spiral and we were all being graphed. The 90's were here again. I took a deep breath and tried to slow my thoughts and put my hand on my friends leg. I said very sincerely and slowly that if we didn't exit immediately that I was going to die.

My drug dealer had sent me about 7 reassuring texts. I missed the days of unapologetic disintegration curled up in the back seat of a car crying about the time you weren't loved. The drastic collapse of the adult drug addict was far less romantic. It's about bills and uncertainty. No time and less energy to recover from the hits that do land. The ghosts in the sky that mingled with the colors and thunder. God bless America.

A short myth on the origins of life

Art (short for Arthur) was once a tiny spherical entity floating in space. Art came into existence not long after the big bang, maybe a few million years or so, when the universe was still all possibility. Many people assume that since they exist on a planet, any other life forms must exist on planets too. Art had never been very close to a planet, he lived in the vacuum of space. Human life relies on the body's processes concerning oxygen to survive. However, oxygen is also a highly corrosive substance, and humans always seem to end up dying. Human life also relies upon converting matter into energy to keep surviving. In order to ingest the right types of matter that are needed to sustain their lives, humans also end up eating a good deal of poisons. Between the oxygen and the bad things in their food, humans can live, but by the very conditions of their life, they also have to die. Art does not eat, or breathe.He lived in a place where there is no oxygen to speak of, nor did he require food when he could live directly on the energy provided to him by a process we would liken it to photosynthesis. Because of this, Art could live forever.

When Art started, it's hard to say exactly what he was. Atoms ran into atoms, and molecules ran into molecules until spontaneously, with no reason that can be explained, they became alive. Those atoms became a self-staining system of energy. Because Art never need die, he had eternity to evolve his own physical definition based on his needs. For a long time, Art remained a wee little speck of dust, because he didn't need to be anything more. When a time came that he was in a particular need to collect more energy to survive, and so he underwent a process that humans might liken to "mitosis," the division of a cell into two like cells. It wasn't reproduction, that clumsy thing came later. There has never been a creature like Art other than Art. It was growth. But, growth worked well for Art, so he kept growing.

Through the course of trial and error, and trial and error, and trial and error, Art shaped himself into the most efficient, effective form for a being of his kind. Art had no need for legs or arms or wings or even organs, really. Art had no purpose but to exist, and he did so beautifully, by forming his cells into a sphere, perfectly shaped, and hollow inside. He would collect light and energy to sustain his life from all sides, from all around him, no matter which way chance happened to take him, and the energy would keep Art alive indefinitely.

After an indeterminate amount of time (determinations of time are all relative, and to my knowledge, have only been determined in relation
to patterns existing on the planet that has come to be called Earth, which did not yet exist), Art came into a large space where he was, for the first time in his life, surrounded by gas. In our language, it was called a nebula. In our eyes, nebulae are enormous bits of fluorescence filled with stars and color and spectacle. When Art arrived in the nebula, with all the light filling him up with energy, he had his first conscious thought. The thought was a chemical reaction to the new environment where he found himself. The
thought was the same thought most of us have whenever we see a photograph of a nebula.

"Beautiful," thought Art.

He swelled, soaking in all the light. It was Art's first feast. Then something else completely new happened. Having entered for the first time an area with a consistent level of gas, Art felt a vibration, the first thing he had ever felt that could be described as sound. For his whole life in the vacuum, nothing had ever been around to communicate sound to him. Now, Art was surrounded by beautiful, glowing matter that stood between him and several stars in the process of being born. The sound Art was experiencing was the rumble of atomic flame, a low roar that could have annihilated him in an instant had he been too near it. But it didn't annihilate him. He kept on
going, and he kept on listening, and again he thought,

"Beautiful."

The roar continued, and the light continued, and after an indeterminate amount of time, until Art left the nebula. Then the roaring continued, and Art ceased to hear it. And he didn't think anymore, because he had no reason to think anymore. And Art kept drifting through space, going wherever inertia and gravity carried him. He had no control over his own motion. He was just a living ball that had done nothing but learn to reproduce, and, twice, he had had thoughts. He followed where gravity took him, until it took him to a place that, in its time, would be called "Earth,"
and a thousand other things.
And Art approached the planet before him, which had a densely packed cloud of gas around it that, in its time, would be called "atmosphere." And as gravity pulled Art in, faster and faster, he came into contact with the sky, and once again, Art could hear. He heard the sound of the air rippling around him as he moved so very fast through it, the roar of the flames developing around him.
And again, he thought,

"Beautiful."

And the energy from the flames fed him, and then the energy from the
flames began to kill him. The parts of his organism that were touching the oxygen first did something that nothing had ever done before: they died. They combined with oxygen and then they died. And then they crumbled away, and a large, living semi sphere was plummeting through the earth's environment. So, without a thought (for Art had never developed the ability to reason, or to plan), Art did what was necessary to survive: all of his cells fled, and Art split up into millions of little pieces, each one now for the
first time individual, but still alive, and they fell upon the earth, and stayed alive. And then they did what Art had taught them to do: they divided, and they grew, and they divided, and they grew.

And they lived.